THIS BOOK BELONGS TO

ANOUCH & YÉVA

FROM MUMMY ♡ 01/20

The Peaceful Lion and the Nagging Crow

A. M. MARCUS

There once was a lion who lived a happy life that was very calm and quiet. Everyone called him The Peaceful Lion.

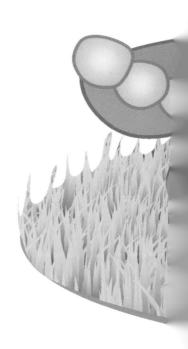

There was also an evil crow that liked to tease and annoy everyone. Everyone called him The Nagging Crow.

One day, the crow saw the lion
sitting peacefully and decided
to see what would happen if he
tried to make the lion angry.

At first, the crow followed the lion around and repeated everything he did, in order to make the lion annoyed.

However, it did not work. The lion paid the crow no attention and did not respond. He stayed as peaceful as ever.

The crow was not going to give up easily, though.

He was determined to make the lion angry. After a few days of thinking about it, he came up with a new plan. He decided to...

Create a lot
of noise...

Make silly faces...

15

Play loud
music...

Shout repeatedly...

He followed this plan for
a while, but it made no
difference. The lion still
remained calm and happy.

Finally, the crow gave up and decided to speak to the lion.

He wanted to know how the lion could stay happy after everything the crow had done to him.

He approached the lion and said, "All this time I have teased you, made silly faces and loud noises, and been very annoying, yet you always stay so happy."

"How do you do that? How do you
remain so calm and peaceful?"

The lion smiled and asked the crow a question. "If someone gave you a gift, who would it belong to?"

"It would be mine,"
the crow replied.

The lion smiled and asked another question. "What if someone tried to give you a gift, but you refused to take it? Who would it belong to then?"

The crow thought carefully and then answered, "I suppose the gift would still belong to the person who tried to give it to me."

The lion nodded,
"Yes! That is right!"

"So, if you decide to give me something, and I refuse it, then it still belongs to you, doesn't it?"

28

The crow paused and thought about this. It was true.

The crow thought silently.
What if I became like The Peaceful Lion?

Whenever someone tries to tease me, annoy me, or hurt my feelings, I would not accept it, and their words would just bounce off me.

Suddenly the crow understood. *Just like the lion, I have a choice. I can choose to be happy, calm, and peaceful, even if someone is trying to make me angry.*

And, if I do not accept any anger, than I will not want to try to make others angry or annoyed either.

The crow thanked the lion for the wonderful lesson he had learned. The lion just nodded, with a wise, knowing look on his smiling face.

After that day, the lion and the crow grew to be good friends, for the crow changed how he treated others and became pleasant to be around.

No one called him The Nagging Crow anymore. Everyone now knew him as The Calm Crow. Together, The Peaceful Lion and the Calm Crow lived happily ever after, and they taught others how to do the same.

Mark's Mystery Message

- ☐ Has anyone ever tried to tease you and make you angry or upset?

- ☐ How did it make you feel?

- ☐ Imagine being A Peaceful Lion, how would you react?

- ☐ How can you respond next time someone tries to annoy you?

 **What Do You Think The Message Is?**

The Message

My Favorite...

FRUIT: Strawberry

SCHOOL SUBJECT: Math

HOBBY: Dancing

 COLOR: Green

ANIMAL: Tiger

SPORT: Soccer

PET: Dog

 **What's Your Favorite?**

For The Grown Ups...

Thank you for sharing this story with your children, I hope you will continue to find it useful as you refer back to it with them when appropriate.

The questions that appear at the end of the story were engineered to be used chronologically to lead the children step by step to take ownership of the message in the quote by Don Miguel Ruiz.

I think we're all guilty of taking things to heart at times so I like to remind myself that most people's actions are about themselves. By showing children how to manage their emotions we can help them to find their inner peace and be immune to the opinions of others as the Lion does in this story. This message can be helpful for children who have been the victim of bullying but it may also help to raise awareness of how we treat others.

If you also enjoyed the message of this story, please consider sharing it with a friend or on social media. Your help in spreading the word is greatly appreciated. Together we can make a huge difference in helping new readers find children's books with powerful messages similar to the one in this story.

If you would like to learn more about me or you have any questions, I would love to hear from you.
You can contact me via my website at <u>ammarcus.com/contact</u> or simply send me an email to <u>assaf@ammarcus.com</u>

My message to the world can be summarised in TWO WORDS.

Visit my website to see what they are 😉

Scan For Your Free Gift

Use the code
01021

ammarcus/free-gift

Printed in Poland
by Amazon Fulfillment
Poland Sp. z o.o., Wrocław

52569876R00026